W9-ATA-654

THE WONDERFUL WIZARD OF OZ COLORING BOOK

[TEXT ABRIDGED]

L. FRANK BAUM

WITH PICTURES BY
W. W. DENSLOW

DOVER PUBLICATIONS, INC., NEW YORK

Planet Friendly Publishing
✓ Made in the United States
✓ Printed on Recycled Paper
Text: 50%   Cover: 10%
Learn more: www.greenedition.org

GREEN EDITION

At Dover Publications we're committed to producing books in an earth-friendly manner and to helping our customers make greener choices.

Manufacturing books in the United States ensures compliance with strict environmental laws and eliminates the need for international freight shipping, a major contributor to global air pollution.

And printing on recycled paper helps minimize our consumption of trees, water and fossil fuels. The text of *The Wonderful Wizard of Oz Coloring Book* was printed on paper made with 50% post-consumer waste, and the cover was printed on paper made with 10% post-consumer waste. According to Environmental Defense's Paper Calculator, by using this innovative paper instead of conventional papers, we achieved the following environmental benefits:

Trees Saved: 25 • Air Emissions Eliminated: 2,346 pounds
Water Saved: 11,295 gallons • Solid Waste Eliminated: 685 pounds

For more information on our environmental practices, please visit us online at www.doverpublications.com/green

Copyright © 1974 by Dover Publications, Inc.
All rights reserved.

The Wonderful Wizard of Oz Coloring Book is a new work, first published by Dover Publications, Inc., in 1974. The text is abridged from the first edition of *The Wonderful Wizard of Oz*, published by the George M. Hill Company in 1900, and the pictures are a selection from W. W. Denslow's illustrations for that edition. The text was abridged especially for this Dover edition.

International Standard Book Number

ISBN-13: 978-0-486-20452-9
ISBN-10: 0-486-20452-9

Manufactured in the
United States by
Courier Corporation
20452925
www.doverpublications.com

OROTHY

LIVED in the midst of the great Kansas prairies, with Uncle Henry, who was a farmer, and Aunt Em, who was the farmer's wife. Their house was small; its one room contained a rusty cooking stove, a cupboard, table, three or four chairs, and two beds. There was no garret, and no cellar—except for the cyclone cellar, a small hole dug into the ground and reached by a trap-door in the middle of the floor, where the family could go in case one of those great whirlwinds arose.

Not a tree nor a house broke the broad sweep of flat country. The sun had baked the plowed land into a gray mass, and even the grass had been burned gray. The house had once been painted, but the sun blistered the paint, and now the house was as dull and gray as everything else.

When Aunt Em came there to live she was a young, pretty wife. The sun and wind had taken the sparkle from her eyes and left them a sober gray. She was thin and gaunt, and never smiled now. When Dorothy, who was an orphan, first came to her, Aunt Em had been so startled by the child's laughter that she would scream and press her hand upon her heart whenever Dorothy's merry voice reached her ears. Uncle Henry was also gray, and worked from morning to night. It was Toto that made Dorothy laugh. He was a little black dog, with small black eyes that twinkled merrily. Dorothy played with him all day, and loved him dearly. Today, however, they were not playing. Uncle Henry sat upon the doorstep and looked anxiously at the sky. Dorothy stood in the door with Toto in her arms. Aunt Em was washing the dishes.

2

From the far north they heard a low wail of the wind, and the long grass bowed in waves before the coming storm. Suddenly Uncle Henry stood up. "There's a cyclone coming," he called; "I'll go look after the stock."

Aunt Em dropped her work. "Quick, Dorothy," she screamed, "run for the cellar!" Toto jumped out of Dorothy's arms and hid under the bed, and the girl started to get him. Aunt Em threw open the trap-door and climbed down into the cellar. Dorothy caught Toto and started to follow her aunt, but the house shook so hard she lost her footing and sat down on the floor.

A strange thing then happened. The house whirled around two or three times and rose slowly through the air. The north and south winds met where the house stood. Now in the center of a cyclone the air is generally still, but the pressure of the wind forced the house to the very top. The wind howled horribly, but Dorothy found she was riding quite easily.

Toto did not like it. He ran around the room barking loudly, and once he fell through the open trap-door, but Dorothy crept to the hole, caught him by the ear, and dragged him into the room again.

Slowly she got over her fright. As the hours passed and nothing terrible happened, she stopped worrying, crawled over the swaying floor to her bed, and fell fast asleep.

She was awakened by a severe shock that might have hurt her if she had not been lying on the soft bed. She sat up and noticed that the house was not moving; nor was it dark, for bright sunshine came in at the window. She opened the door and gave a cry of amazement.

The cyclone had set the house down, very gently—for a cyclone—in the midst of a country of marvelous beauty. There were lovely patches of green sward all about, with stately trees bearing luscious fruits. Birds with brilliant plumage sang amidst banks of gorgeous flowers. A small brook nearby sounded very cheerful to the little girl who had lived so long on the dry, gray prairies.

Coming toward her were four of the queerest-looking people she had ever seen. They were not as big as the grown people she had always been used to; they were about her size, but considerably older. The three men were dressed all in blue, from their boots to their pointed hats. The little woman, who was dressed all in white, bowed before Dorothy and said, "You are welcome, most noble Sorceress, to the land of the Munchkins. We are grateful to you for having killed the Wicked Witch of the East, and for setting our people free from bondage." Dorothy listened in wonder; she was just a harmless little girl, she told them, who had never killed anyone.

"Your house did, anyway, and that is the same thing. See! there are her two toes, still sticking out from the block of wood."

Dorothy gave a cry of fright. There, indeed, just under the corner of the house, were two feet sticking out, shod in silver shoes. "Who was she?" asked Dorothy.

"She was the Wicked Witch of the East, who has held all the Munchkins—" she pointed to the three little men, who bowed—"in bondage. When they saw she was dead, they sent a swift messenger to me; I am the Witch of the North."

"But I thought all witches were wicked," said Dorothy.

"Oh no; that is a great mistake. There were only four witches in all the Land of Oz, and two of them, those who live in the North and South, are good witches. Those who dwelt in the East and West were indeed wicked, and now, there is only one Wicked Witch in all the land of Oz—the one who lives in the West."

"But my Aunt Em—from Kansas—said the witches were all dead."

"I do not know where Kansas is—is it a civilized country?" Dorothy nodded. "That explains it. You see, the Land of Oz has never been civilized; therefore we still have witches and wizards."

"Who are the wizards?" Dorothy asked.

"Oz himself is the great Wizard—he is more powerful than the rest of us. He lives in the City of Emeralds."

One of the Munchkins noticed that the feet of the Wicked Witch had completely dried up and disappeared, leaving only her silver shoes. The little woman laughed. "She was so old, she dried up quickly in the sun. But the shoes are yours; there is a charm connected with them."

After putting the shoes away, Dorothy said, "I am anxious to get back to my aunt and uncle, for I am sure they will worry about me. Can you help me find my way?"

The Munchkins looked at each other and shook their heads. To the north, east, south, and west, they said, was a great desert impossible to cross. The west was especially bad, since the Wicked Witch of the West would make Dorothy her slave if she went that way. "You must go to the City of Emeralds," the little woman said. "Perhaps Oz will help you."

"Is he a good man?" asked Dorothy anxiously.

"He is a good wizard. Whether he is a man or not, I cannot tell, for I have never seen him. It is a long journey, through a country that is sometimes dark and terrible. I cannot come with you, but I will give you my kiss, and no one will dare to hurt a person who has been kissed by the Witch of the North." Where her lips touched they left a round, shining mark. "The road to Emerald City is paved with yellow brick, so you cannot miss it." With that she waved, whirled on her heel, and disappeared.

The next morning Dorothy put on her white-and-blue gingham dress, her pink sunbonnet, and filled a little basket with bread from the cupboard. Then she noticed how old and worn her shoes were, and remembered the silver shoes belonging to the Witch of the East. They were a perfect fit—just the thing for a long walk.

"Come along, Toto," she said, "we will go to Emerald City and ask the great Oz how to get back to Kansas again."

There were several roads nearby, and it did not take her long to find the one paved with yellow brick. The sun shone bright and the birds were singing, and her silver shoes tinkled merrily on the yellow brick roadway. She did not feel as bad as you might think a little girl would who had suddenly been swooped up and set down in the midst of a strange land.

She was surprised to see how pretty the country was. There were neat fences and domed houses all painted blue, since in Munchkin land blue was the favorite color.

Soon she thought she would stop to rest, and climbed over a fence into a great cornfield where a Scarecrow had been placed high on a pole to keep the birds away. The Scarecrow's head was a small sack stuffed with straw, with eyes, nose and mouth painted on to represent a face. An old, pointed blue hat was perched on this head, and the rest of the figure was a blue suit stuffed with straw. As Dorothy gazed into its painted face, she was surprised to see one of the eyes slowly wink at her.

13

She thought she must have been mistaken, for none of the scarecrows in Kansas ever winked at her.

"Good day," he said, in a rather husky voice.

"Did you speak?" asked the girl, in wonder.

"Certainly. How do you do?"

"I'm pretty well, thank you," replied Dorothy politely; "how do you do?"

"I'm not feeling well, for it is tedious being perched up here night and day with this pole up my back. If you will take away the pole I shall be greatly obliged."

Dorothy reached up both arms and lifted the figure off the pole; being stuffed with straw, he was quite light. "Thank you very much," said the Scarecrow, "I feel like a new man." He asked Dorothy why she was there, and she explained she was going to the Emerald City, to ask the great Oz to send her back to Kansas. She was surprised that he had never heard of Emerald City, or been there.

"I don't know anything," he explained. "You see, I am
stuffed, so I have no brains at all. Do you think if I went
with you, Oz would give me some brains?"

"Even if he didn't you could not be any worse off than
you are," Dorothy said. "I'll ask him to do all he can." The
Scarecrow was very grateful, but somewhat nervous
about Toto, who kept sniffing his straw. "He never bites,"
Dorothy said.

"I'm not afraid," the Scarecrow said. "I'm only afraid of one thing—a lighted match!" As they walked along, he told her he had been put together by a Munchkin farmer only recently, and knew nothing of the world until the farmer had painted in a pair of eyes and ears for him. But the farmer put him in a field and forgot about him. When the Scarecrow discovered he could not even scare crows away, he saw he was a complete failure. That's when he had decided to go get some brains. "It is such an uncomfortable feeling to know one is a fool!"

Toward evening they came to a great forest. The Scarecrow, being straw, was not tired at all, but Dorothy was, so when they came to a little cottage in the trees, she slept on a bed of dried leaves while the Scarecrow stood guard all night.

The next morning Dorothy and the Scarecrow had started back to the yellow-brick road when they heard a deep groan nearby. The sound seemed to come from behind them, and they turned and were walking through the forest toward something shiny among the trees when Dorothy let out a cry of surprise.

One of the trees had been partially chopped through, and beside it, with a raised ax, was a man made entirely of tin. His head and arms were jointed to his body, but he stood perfectly motionless. "Did you groan?" asked Dorothy.

"Yes, I did. I've been groaning for more than a year, and no one has ever heard me." He told Dorothy to get the oil-can on the shelf in his cottage. "My joints are rusted so badly I cannot move them."

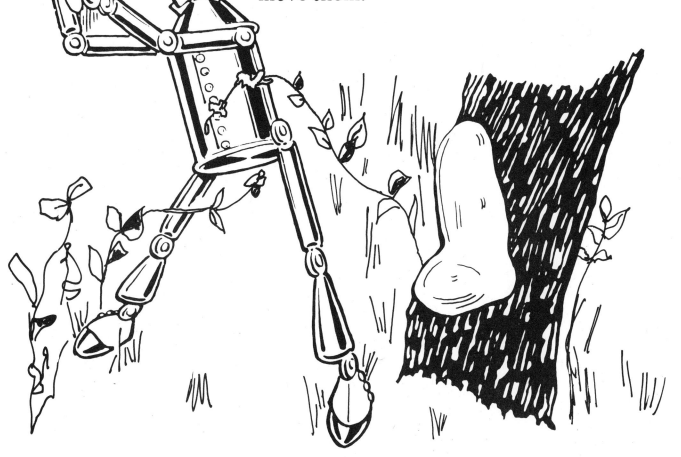

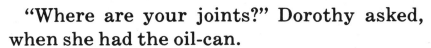

"Where are your joints?" Dorothy asked, when she had the oil-can.

"Oil my neck first." The Scarecrow helped to move it gently from side to side. "Now the joints in my arms." When she was finished, the Tin Woodman gave a grateful sigh of satisfaction and leaned against a tree. They had certainly saved his life, he said; why were they here? Dorothy explained their reasons for going to see the Wizard.

The Woodman thought a moment, then he said, "Do you suppose Oz would give me a heart?"

"It would be as easy as to give the Scarecrow brains."

"Then I'll join you." They were all delighted to have a new friend. Before they left for the yellow-brick road, however, the Woodman asked Dorothy to put the oil-can in her basket. "If it should rain, I'd need it badly." He was able to help clear a path through the forest for them with his ax.

As they walked along, he told
them he had been a woodman's
son who had unintentionally angered the Wicked Witch of
the East; the Witch had then enchanted his ax so that it
would turn against him. When it cut off his left leg, a
tinsmith made him a new one; the same for his right. But
when the ax split him in half, he needed a whole body of
tin, and they left out a heart. The tin body shone nicely in
the sun and could not be damaged by the ax; unfortunate-
ly he had been caught in a rainstorm the year before when
he did not have his oil-can handy. During the year he had
stood there he had had time to think, and it was then he
decided to go get a heart.

"I would rather have brains," the Scarecrow said; "for a fool like me would not know what to do with a heart if he had one."

"I shall take the heart," the Tin Woodman replied; "for brains do not make one happy, and happiness is the best thing in the world."

Dorothy did not know which of her friends was right. What worried her was that the bread was nearly gone, and she was rather glad that neither the Woodman nor the Scarecrow ever ate anything.

All this time Dorothy and her companions had been
walking through the thick woods where every now and
then came a deep growl from some animal hidden in the
trees. "How long do you think it will be," Dorothy asked
the Woodman, "before we are out of the forest?"

He said he didn't know, he'd never been to Emerald City.
"I am not afraid, though, so long as I have my oil-can,
while nothing can hurt the Scarecrow, and you bear upon
your forehead the mark of the Good Witch's kiss."

"But Toto! What will protect him?"

"We must protect him ourselves, if he is in danger," said
the Tin Woodman.

Just then there came a terrible roar from the forest, and the next moment a great Lion bounded into the road. With one blow he sent the Scarecrow spinning and struck at the Tin Woodman with his sharp claws. Toto ran barking toward the Lion, and when it opened its great mouth to bite the dog, Dorothy, heedless of danger, rushed forward and slapped the Lion upon his nose. "Don't you dare bite Toto! You ought to be ashamed of yourself, a big beast like you, to bite a poor little dog."

"I didn't bite him."

"No, but you tried to. You're nothing but a big coward."

"I know it. I've always known it," he said, hanging his head in shame. "How can I help it?"

"To strike a stuffed man—" she said, patting the Scarecrow into shape.

"Is he stuffed? That's why he went over so easily. Is the other one stuffed, also?"

"No, he's made of tin."

"That's why he blunted my claws. When they scratched against the tin it made a cold shiver run down my back. Is the dog made of tin or stuffed?"

"Neither. He's a—a—a meat dog."

"No one would think of biting such a little thing except a coward like me." Dorothy asked him what made him such a coward. "I suppose I was born that way," he said. "All the other animals expected me to be brave, for the Lion is everywhere thought to be the King of Beasts.

If the elephants and the tigers and bears had ever fought back, I should have run away—but as soon as they heard me roar they all tried to get away from me. It's my great sorrow," he said, wiping a tear from his eye with the tip of his tail.

They explained that they were going to see the Wizard to get brains for the Scarecrow and a heart for the Tin Woodman. "Do you think Oz would give me courage?" They said they thought so. "Then I'll go, for my life has been simply unbearable without a bit of courage."

The next morning they came to a field of beautiful
flowers. There were big yellow and white and blue and
purple blossoms, so brilliant they almost dazzled Dorothy's eyes. "Aren't they beautiful?" she asked, as she
breathed in the spicy scent. Soon they were in the midst of
a great meadow of red poppies.

Now it is well known that when there are many poppies
together their odor is so powerful that anyone who
breathes it falls asleep, and if not removed would sleep
there forever. But Dorothy did not know this; her eyes
grew heavy, and although the Scarecrow and Tin Woodman urged her to hurry, she could resist the flowers no
longer. She fell among the poppies, fast asleep. "What
shall we do?" said the Tin Woodman.

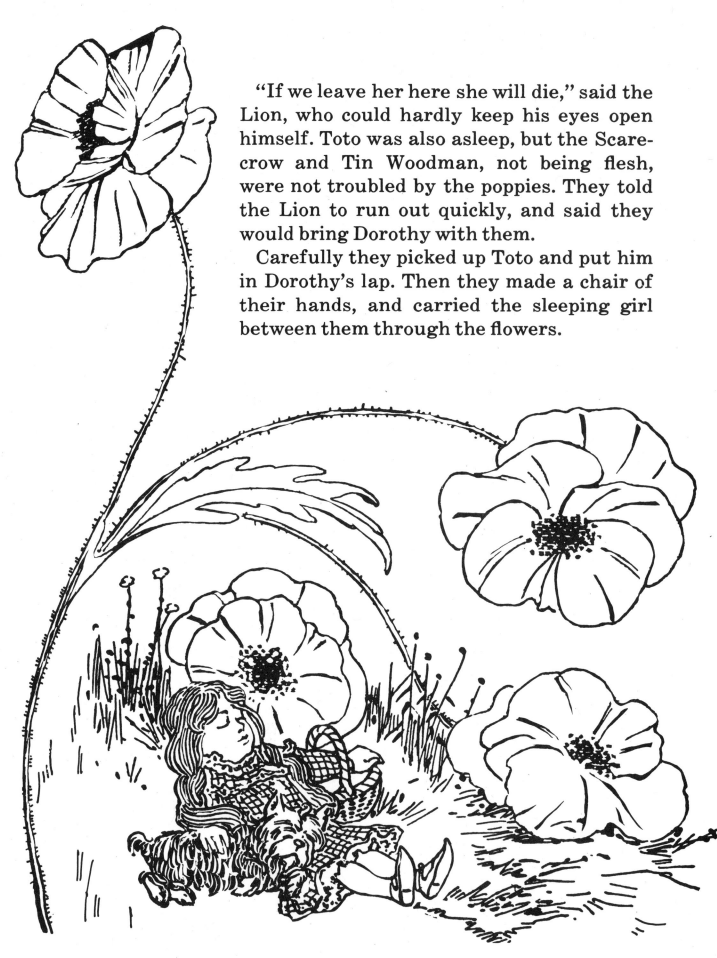

"If we leave her here she will die," said the Lion, who could hardly keep his eyes open himself. Toto was also asleep, but the Scarecrow and Tin Woodman, not being flesh, were not troubled by the poppies. They told the Lion to run out quickly, and said they would bring Dorothy with them.

Carefully they picked up Toto and put him in Dorothy's lap. Then they made a chair of their hands, and carried the sleeping girl between them through the flowers.

On and on they walked, and finally placed the girl in a pretty spot, near the river, far enough from the poppy field to prevent her breathing any more of the poison.

When Dorothy awoke, she was surprised to find herself lying on the grass, and she breathed deeply of the sweet, fresh air. Toto was already awake, and when the Lion shortly joined them, their spirits rose and they decided they should hurry back to find the road that would carry them to Emerald City. Soon they were on the yellow-brick road again, glad to be out of the forest and away from danger. They saw green fences and little green houses, and people dressed in peaked hats and lovely emerald-colored clothing. "We must be near Emerald City," said Dorothy.

They told one family in one of the houses they were going to see the great Oz. "Are you sure he will see you?" the woman said. "He never goes out and never lets anyone into his presence." Dorothy asked what he was like. "It's hard to tell. Some say he's like a bird, some say like an elephant."

It all sounded very strange, but there was nothing to do but go on. Soon they came to the great green wall that surrounded the city, and when they came to a big gate, studded with emeralds, Dorothy rang the bell.

The door swung slowly open, and before them was a Gate-Keeper clothed all in green. They explained that they

had come to see the great Oz, and the man was so surprised he sat down to think about it. "It has been years since anyone asked to see Oz," he said. "He is powerful and terrible, and if you come on an idle errand, he can destroy you in an instant." He would take them to the Palace, the man said, but first they must each put on green spectacles— to keep the glory of Emerald City from blinding them.

Since he insisted, they let the Gate-Keeper fit each of them—even Toto—with a pair of green spectacles which he then locked into place. Afterwards he led them through the portal into the streets of the city.

The streets of Emerald City were lined with green houses studded with emeralds, and Dorothy and her friends found them dazzling.

Even the sky above had a green tint. The people, who all wore green clothing, seemed pleasant and friendly, but kept their distance when they saw the Lion.

When a soldier opened the door to the Palace of Oz, he was told that these four wished to see the Wizard. Soon the soldier returned and said Oz would see them, one at a time, one day each. "Did you see the Wizard?" they asked.

"No one has ever seen Oz. He sat behind a screen and I gave him your message." Oz had decided to see them, they learned, upon hearing of Dorothy's silver shoes.

In the meantime, they were given comfortable rooms in the Palace. Dorothy was pleased to see that hers had a green fountain that shot green perfume into the air.

The next morning she put on one of the beautiful green dresses in the wardrobe, and followed the soldier to the Throne Room of Oz. She found herself in a big, round room with a high arched roof, and a throne in the center, on which was an enormous Head, with no body to support it, bigger than the head of the biggest giant.

"I am Oz," the lips said, "the Great and Terrible. Who are you, and why do you seek me?"

"I am Dorothy," she said, as bravely as possible, "the Small and Meek. I came to ask you to send me back to Kansas, where my Aunt Em and Uncle Henry are."

The Head wanted to know where she got the silver shoes, and she told him about killing the Wicked Witch of the East. "Very well," the Head went on, "kill the Wicked Witch of the West for me, and I will send you back to Kansas, not before."

Dorothy began to weep. "I never killed anything, willingly. If you, who are Great and Terrible, cannot kill her yourself, how do you expect me to do it?"

"I do not know, but that is my answer. Remember that the Witch is terribly Wicked, and ought to be killed."

Sorrowfully Dorothy went back and told the Lion and the Scarecrow and the Tin Woodman what Oz had said. That night she lay down on her green bed and cried herself to sleep.

The next three days the Scarecrow, the Tin Woodman, and the Lion all saw the Wizard—but each saw him in a different way. To the Scarecrow, he seemed almost kindly; to the Tin Woodman, a terrible beast; to the Lion, a horrifying ball of fire. With each, he promised to give them what they desired—brains, a heart, or courage—but only after they helped Dorothy destroy the Wicked Witch of the West.

"I will go with you," the Lion told Dorothy, "but I'm too much of a coward to kill the Witch."

"I will go too," declared the Scarecrow; "but I shall not be of much help to you, I am such a fool."

"I haven't the heart to harm even a Witch," replied the Tin Woodman; "but if you go I shall certainly go with you."

They decided to start the next morning, so in the meantime the Tin Woodman had his joints oiled, the Scarecrow stuffed himself with fresh straw, and the people of Emerald City gave them nourishing things to eat.

The next morning at the Gate, when the Gate-Keeper took back their green spectacles, they asked him which road led to the Wicked Witch of the West. He shook with fear. "There is no road," he said, "because no one ever wanted to go that way. But go to the West, into the country of the Winkies, and *she* will find *you.*"

"We mean to destroy her," said the Scarecrow.

"Well, take care; for she is wicked and fierce and may not let you destroy her."

They turned toward the West, and were surprised to see that things were no longer green but yellow; even Dorothy's green dress had changed color. The country became rougher, and after passing through a thick wood, where the trees seemed almost to lift them from the ground and shake them, they came to an open area, where Dorothy, exhausted, sat down and fell asleep.

Now the Wicked Witch of the West had but one eye, yet that was as powerful as a telescope and could see anything. So, as she sat in the door of her castle, she could see Dorothy asleep, with her friends about her. Angrily she took a Golden Cap from her cupboard; whoever owned this cap could command the Winged Monkeys. Standing on her left foot she said "Ep-pe, pep-pe, kak-ke!" Immediately the sky was darkened and she was surrounded by a crowd of Monkeys, each with a pair of immense and powerful wings on his shoulders. "Destroy them!" she said.

The Monkeys swooped down on the group, with their long, hairy arms stretched out and their ugly faces grinning. They knocked the Scarecrow and Tin Woodman about, tied up the Lion with ropes, and would have hurt Dorothy if they had not seen the mark of the Good Witch's kiss on her forehead. "We dare not harm this girl," they said. "We can only carry her to the castle of the Wicked Witch and leave her there."

In the Witch's castle, the Wicked Witch began to tremble when she saw the mark on Dorothy's forehead and the Silver Shoes she was wearing. The Witch had always wanted those powerful shoes for herself. She sensed, however, that Dorothy did not herself know their power. "I can make her my slave," the Witch thought. "Now do everything I say," she told Dorothy, "or I will make an end of you."

Soon Dorothy was cleaning the pots and pans and mopping the floor in the halls that were constantly guarded by the yellow Winkies, the Witch's slaves. The Witch meanwhile was plotting how to get Dorothy's shoes. Her best chance was when Dorothy took a bath, but the Witch had a horrible dread of water and kept her distance. Once Toto caught her trying to get the shoes and bit her leg bravely, but it did not even bleed, the Witch was so evil. Dorothy meanwhile worried about her friends and cried constantly at the thought of not getting to Kansas to see her Aunt Em again.

Finally the Witch thought of a trick to trip Dorothy while she was mopping the floor one day. The Witch grabbed one of the Silver Shoes when it fell off. "Give me back my shoe!" Dorothy said. "I shall keep it," the Witch said, "and soon get the other one!"

This made Dorothy so very angry that she picked up a bucket of water and dashed it over the Witch, wetting her from head to foot. Instantly the wicked woman gave a loud cry of fear; and then began to shrink and fall away. "See what you've done!" she screamed. "In a minute I shall melt away."

"I'm very sorry, indeed," said Dorothy, who was truly frightened to see the Witch actually melting away like brown sugar before her eyes.

"Didn't you know water would be the end of me?" Dorothy shook her head. "Well, in a few minutes I shall be all melted, and you will have the castle to yourself. I have

been wicked in my day, but I never thought a little girl like you would ever be able to melt me and end my wicked deeds. Look out—here I go!"

With these words the Witch fell down in a brown, melted, shapeless mass and began to spread over the clean boards of the kitchen floor. Seeing that she had really melted away to nothing, Dorothy drew another bucket of water and threw it over the mess. She then swept it all out the door. After picking up the silver shoe, which was all that was left of the old woman, she put it on her foot again. Then she ran out to the court-yard to tell the yellow Winkies they were no longer slaves.

The Winkies were delighted to hear that the Witch had been melted away, and the Scarecrow, Tin Woodman and Cowardly Lion (now free of his ropes) wept tears of joy to have their little friend with them again. But the Tin Woodman was badly dented from his struggles against the Winged Monkeys, and the Scarecrow had lost much straw. The first act of the free Winkies was to solder the Tin Woodman together again and sew up the Scarecrow, so

that they were as good as new. Then they outfitted the
group for their journey, so that they could go back and tell
Oz they had done as commanded, and had killed the
Wicked Witch of the West.

At the thought of the long way to the Emerald City,
however, where there was no road, Dorothy and her
friends were thrown into despair. It seemed impossible to
get there! Then she remembered the Golden Cap of the
Wicked Witch and read the words she found in the lining.
When she said aloud "Ep-pe, pep-pe, kak-ke" she was
surrounded by the Winged Monkeys. They, like the Winkies, were a good people who had fallen into the clutches of
the Wicked Witch.

The Monkeys told her they would gladly take them there, and Dorothy, the Scarecrow, the Woodman, the Lion, and Toto were each seized by a Winged Monkey on either side, and flown, squirming uneasily, to the Emerald City.

There the Gate-Keeper seemed surprised to see them, but tied on their green spectacles and said he would tell the Wizard they had returned. For some reason, the Wizard kept them waiting several days. At last, when they insisted upon seeing him, they were allowed into his presence. They wondered what shape Oz would take, but this time he was only a Voice, intoning solemnly "I am Oz, the Great and Terrible. Why do you seek me?"

"We have come to claim our promise, O Oz," Dorothy said.

"What promise?"

"You promised to send me back to Kansas when the Wicked Witch was destroyed. I melted her with a bucket of water."

"Dear me, how sudden! Well, come tomorrow, and I will think it over."

"You've had plenty of time already," said the Tin Woodman. At this point the Lion let out a roar, and Toto, frightened, knocked over a screen that stood in one corner. The next moment they were all filled with wonder. There, standing in the spot where the screen had been, was a little old man with a bald head and wrinkled face. "Who are you?" said the Tin Woodman. "I am Oz, the Great and Terrible."

"I thought you were a great Head," said Dorothy. "Or a Ball of Fire," said the Lion. "That was only make-believe," he said, showing them the disguises he had used. "I'm just a common man."

"You're a humbug," said the Scarecrow.

"Exactly so," he said, "a humbug! But no one knows it but you four—and myself." He had been, he said, a balloonist from Omaha, Nebraska ("Why, that's near Kansas," Dorothy said). One day his balloon had been carried high over the clouds until it had come down in this wonderful country. Everyone thought he was a Wizard, landing that way, and he had encouraged them, building this city and telling everyone it was green and making them wear green spectacles so that it really was. But he had not intended any harm. His only fear was of the Wicked Witches, and hearing Dorothy had killed the Witch of the East, he thought she could kill the Witch of the West.

"But your promises—" Dorothy said, near to tears. "How will I get back to Kansas, and the Scarecrow get his brains, and the Tin Woodman his heart, and the Cowardly Lion his courage? I think you are a very bad man."

"Oh, no, my dear; I'm really a very good man; but I'm a very bad Wizard."

"Can't you give me brains?" asked the Scarecrow.

"You don't need them. You are learning something every day. A baby has brains, but it doesn't know much."

"How about my courage?" said the Lion.

"All you need is confidence in yourself. There is no living thing that is not afraid when it faces danger. True courage is in facing danger when you are afraid, and that kind of courage you have in plenty."

"How about my heart?" asked the Tin Woodman.

"Why, as for that, I think you are wrong to want a heart. It makes most people unhappy. If you only knew it, you are in luck not to have a heart."

But the three of them insisted, and he said he would fulfill their wishes in the morning.

The next morning the Scarecrow went to the Wizard to get his brains (although Dorothy told him she liked him as he was). "You must excuse me," the Wizard said, "if I take your head off." Then, taking it to a back room, he mixed up some bran and poured it in, in place of the straw. "Hereafter you will be a great man, for I have given you a lot of bran-new brains." The Scarecrow then had wonderful thoughts which he never told anyone, since no one could understand them but himself.

The Tin Woodman came next to get his heart. "I shall have to cut a hole in your breast," the Wizard said. Having cut a small, square opening, he inserted a pretty heart made entirely of silk and stuffed with sawdust. "Is it a kind heart?" the Woodman asked. "It's a heart any man would be proud of," the Wizard said. The Tin Woodman was happy to hear his new heart rattle as he walked out.

When the Lion came, next, for his courage, the Wizard reached up to a high shelf and took down a square green bottle. He poured some out for the Lion and said, "Drink it." "What is it?" "Well," Oz said, "if it were inside of you, it would be courage." The Lion drank deeply. "How do you feel now?" "Full of courage," said the Lion as he went to rejoin his friends.

Thus the Wizard took care of the wishes of the Scarecrow, the Tin Woodman, and the Lion. But he was not sure how he could get Dorothy back to Kansas again.

Four days later the Wizard told Dorothy he had a plan for leaving Oz. The hard thing was to cross the desert; however, he could make a balloon from the silk in the palace, and float it on hot air from a bonfire which the Tin Woodman could make. Dorothy was pleased to hear that Oz planned to go back with her. "I'm tired of being a humbug," he said. "I'd rather go back to Omaha and be in a circus again."

It took three days to make the balloon, and all the people then gathered round to see the great event. The Tin Woodman's fire was already roaring, and the Wizard was in the balloon, telling everyone "While I'm away, the Scarecrow will rule over you. Come, Dorothy; hurry, or the balloon will fly away."

But Dorothy could not find Toto; by the time she picked him up and started toward the balloon, crack, went the ropes and the balloon rose without her. "Come back," she shouted, "I want to go too."

"I can't come back, my dear," called Oz from the balloon. "Good-bye!"

"Good-bye," everyone called, and all eyes watched him rise and disappear into the sky. It was the last they saw of Oz, and no one knew whether he reached Omaha or not....

Dorothy wept bitterly at the passing of her hope of getting home to Kansas again, though she forgave the Wizard, for he had certainly done his best.

"Why not stay in Oz with us?" the Scarecrow said. He was the Ruler now because of his brains, and the Tin Woodman and the Lion would be given positions suitable for one with such a fine heart and one with such splendid courage.

"But I don't want to live here," cried Dorothy. "I want to go to Kansas, and live with my Aunt Em and Uncle Henry."

"Well, then, what can be done?" said the Woodman.

It was Glinda the Good, however, who was to tell Dorothy how she could get back to Kansas. Incredibly beautiful, her dress pure white, she leaned down toward Dorothy and looked at her with her kindly blue eyes. "What can I do for you, my child?" she said.

Dorothy told the beautiful Glinda all her story; how the cyclone had brought her to the Land of Oz, how she had found her companions, and of the wonderful adventures they had met with. She told of the finding of the Golden Cap, which she gave now to Glinda. "My greatest wish," Dorothy added, "is to get

back to Kansas, for Aunt Em will surely think something dreadful has happened to me."

Glinda kissed the face of the young girl. "Bless your dear heart," she said. "Your Silver Shoes will carry you back to Kansas. If you had known their power you could have gone back to Aunt Em the very first day."

"But then I should not have had my wonderful brains!" cried the Scarecrow. "I might have passed my whole life in the farmer's cornfield."

"And I should not have had my lovely heart," said the Tin Woodman. "I might have stood and rusted in the forest till the end of the world."

"And I should have lived a coward forever," declared the Lion, "and no beast of the forest would have had a good word to say to me."

"This is all true," said Dorothy, "and I am glad I was of use to these good friends. But now that each of them has had what he most desired, I think I should like to go back to Kansas."

"All you have to do is to knock the heels together three times and command the shoes to carry you wherever you wish to go."

"If that is so," said the child, joyfully, "I will ask them to carry me back to Kansas at once."

She threw her arms around the Lion's neck and kissed him, patting his big head tenderly. Then she kissed the Tin Woodman, who was weeping in a way most dangerous to his joints. But she hugged the soft, stuffed body of the Scarecrow in her arms instead of kissing his painted face, and found she was crying herself at this sorrowful parting from her loving comrades.

Glinda kissed her a good-bye kiss. Then Dorothy took Toto in her arms, said one more farewell to her friends, clapped her heels together saying, "Take me home to Aunt Em!"

Instantly she was whirling through the air swiftly in her Silver Shoes, and then she stopped so suddenly she rolled over upon the grass several times before she knew where she was. "Good gracious!" she cried. She was sitting on the broad Kansas prairie, and there was the new farm house Uncle Henry built after the cyclone had carried away the old one.

Uncle Henry was milking the cows, and Toto began barking joyously to see him. When Dorothy started to run she found she was in her stocking feet; the Silver Shoes had fallen off in her flight, and were lost forever....

Aunt Em had just come out to water the cabbages when she looked up and saw Dorothy running toward her. "My darling child!" she cried, folding the little girl in her arms and covering her face with kisses; "where in the world did you come from?"

"From the Land of Oz," said Dorothy, gravely. "And here is Toto, too. And, oh, Aunt Em! I'm so glad to be at home again!"